COWBOYS' MAFIA AGE GAP

Fertile for the Kingpin Story

Leandra Camilli

ISBN: 9798796908686
Imprint: Independently published

1st edition

Cover design by: Leandra Camilli

CONTENTS

CHAPTER 1

I was shifting some documents over on the table when I felt a pair of hands settling on my waist. I turned my head around at the same moment, finding the eyes of one of the mafiosos.

He came here not too long ago, and I thought he'd already left. His hands were big. I could feel that just by the way he had them positioned near my butt.

I parted my legs right away, even though I was fighting not to.

"Something I can help you with?" He asked, making me feel nervous, but not just thanks to the age gap. Glancing over his face, his wrinkles and chicken legs didn't lie. He was at least 10 years older than me, which meant that I didn't even have the same amount of experience as him when it came to sex.

"I'm just trying to find something," I responded, trying to move my body so that the front of it was facing him, but his hands weren't allowing me to. And his hands not budging meant that I couldn't do that. Trapped, all I could feel was his heavy breathing.

My eyes shifting down, I couldn't help but take a gander at his lips. They were perfect, not too thin or thick. Just perfect. I couldn't help but imagine myself kissing them, lips rubbing over each other, his tongue coming in and infecting me.

His hand touched my chin, snapping me back to reality.

"And what are you trying to find?" He quizzed, his hand moving down and settling on my neck. For a moment, I thought he was going to grab it, but he was only keeping it there.

Thank goodness, I thought, letting a cloud of air come out through my nostrils. He wasn't going to kill me. Not yet. He was a mafioso, but he wasn't a killer.

I bit my lower lip. No point in giving away my cover and taking down my own mask. I came here with a mission, and I was going to see it through.

"Can you please just-" I tried saying, moving away from him, but then his fingers dug deeper into my skin. He was keeping me pinned in place, and there was nothing I could do about it. I couldn't do anything because my pussy was getting more lubricated as the seconds passed, time moving too slow for my liking.

I couldn't deny that, as someone who was a spy and hadn't had her first time yet, being this close to a man made me feel nervous and scared. I didn't know what his intentions were, just that he suspected something was up.

He was so close to me that I could sniff the minty breath coming out of his mouth. It was like this man was doing it on purpose. He was even keeping his lips parted, which was something nobody ever did, unless they were using it in their favor.

"No point in lying to me or escaping me again," he murmured, moving his hand up and under my shirt. Gliding it further up, I couldn't help but stiffen my body when he was inches away from scraping over my breast.

My nipple was hard and perky, ready to give away what I was thinking about him and the fact that he was my crush.

"I wasn't trying to escape from you," I barked, trying to push him off me again, but finding the same obstacle from before. He pressed his fingers more tightly into my skin, keeping me where I was.

His eyes were staring into mine like he was reading my mind, his fingers moving further up until they were kneading my boob.

"I said – and I'm not going to repeat myself – that you shouldn't try to lie to me. It's not good for you," he affirmed, raising his voice and making it the boom in the darkness of the room. Otis and Walter weren't here, as else they would be doing something about this.

The man standing in front of me wasn't even their only guest. He was just one of the two who came here.

I should be fighting back with more impetus than I was, but my crush over him was stronger than I thought. My skin was hot and cold at the same time, sweat pooling on my forehead.

He opened his hand so that it was cupping my boob, the corners of his lips stretching to form a smile.

I parted my lips, my eyes closing slightly. I was giving myself up for him, letting him do whatever he wanted with me. As he applied pressure with his fingers against my boob, a moan escaped my lips. Smiling again, he lowered his head until his lips started to press against mine.

I should be biting his lips, but I wasn't. It wasn't even a strong, determined kiss that should be melting me. Rather, it was slow and sensual, showing me that this mafioso was taking his time.

His hand moved further up, fingers interlacing around my nipple. Pressing against it, he made me moan. Waves of heat were building up in my body, making me feel as if I was next to a volcano. Sweat was pooling on my forehead, soaking me.

He pulled his head back, looking into my eyes. "Such a pity that you aren't like them. You would make such a great addition to the team. We need more girls like you in the herd."

I blinked twice, not understanding what he was trying to say. He pulled his hand back, trotting away from me. The moment he wasn't breathing all the air in the room anymore, I felt that I could finally breathe again.

Stepping toward the door, he settled his hand on the doorframe, turning his head so that he could peek over his shoulder. "I expect to see you at the barn tonight, at midnight. Be there so that I don't have to tell anyone about you and what you came here to do."

And despite having the option of just running away, I decided to bite the bait.

CHAPTER 2

Turning my head from side to side, I couldn't help but feel butterflies flying about in my stomach. I was in the barn, but it was empty. Not only was it dark, but it was also eerie and I couldn't hear anything either inside it or outside of it. My hands went up to my chest, like I was trying to protect myself from that Italian mafioso.

A twig snapping outside the barn made me whirl around, finding out that a huge man was coming into the barn from behind me. But it wasn't just one man – it was two who were stepping toward me like this was a normal encounter.

One of them closed the door of the barn, everything around me becoming black. I felt a hand settling on my shoulder, his fingers moving under the shirt. He pulled it down, revealing my torso.

My bra was still protecting my breasts from his hungry eyes, but even that wasn't going to remain where it was for long.

"Allow me, pretty little thing," someone behind me hissed, his fingers snapping the bra and pulling it off me. My arms crossed over my chest at the same moment, and I felt colder.

Something pressed against my neck, making me squirm. It was one of the Italian mafiosos, his hands settling on my love handles and pressing his crotch against my ass.

I felt my asscheeks pushing up closer to him, willing him to come inside me. Was he going to do that? I didn't know, but the thought lingered in my mind still.

I couldn't believe we were doing this at the barn. Such a dirty, dusty place, and yet, it still felt right that it was happening here. I couldn't imagine myself doing this anywhere else.

"How are you feeling? Want me to come inside?" The cowboy purred into my ear, his hands groping my shoulders and roaming over my arms. Did he even have to ask? The answer was obvious.

I nodded when he asked, "Then tell me what you were looking for in the room. I want to know everything, and so do Walter and Otis."

I moaned, his fingers pulling down my jeans as he forced me to step out of them. Putting a hand over my shoulder, he pressed it forward, making me bend down and then get on my knees on the soil.

He forced it further, and now I was with my hands on the floor, ass pointing up. One of his hands roamed over my asscheeks, like he was delimiting his territory. A zipper opened in front of me, and a pair of pants fell to the ground.

Eros looped his fingers around his shaft, pointing it at me. It was right in front of my face, looking mean and ferocious.

Once it was inside of me, I knew he would have no mercy. He would pound it in and out of me, turning me into one of those things. I was going to become a hucow like them...

"Please... Have mercy," I pleaded, a smile creeping up on his face.

"I don't think I will," Eros said, putting his hand on the back of my head and pulling it down with force, forcing me to open my mouth right away. I felt his cock barging inside me, stretching my lips and then getting lodged where my throat was.

All I could do was to lick the lower part of his bulbous cockhead, willing him to be as merciful with me as he could. His smile widening, I knew that things weren't going to be so simple.

He pressed his hand against my head and then pulled it up, repeating the process over and over.

Pain started to shoot through my body, making me groan and moan. I never thought it was possible to feel so much pain.

His cock scraped over my tongue, hit against the back of my throat, and created friction against my lips, making me feel like I was going to pass out.

His fingers were grabbing my hair hard, the pace at which he was shoving my head up and down increasing. The heat inside my body started to build up and then it washed over me, making me moan as my orgasm surged.

Just as that happened, his dick started to throb and convulse inside my mouth. It wasn't long until he was coming inside of it, rewarding me with his salty and creamy release.

Eros was potent, his milk making me wonder what it would be like if he were creaming inside my womb.

His dick stopped convulsing, calming down. One last drop of his milk broke off and fell to my tongue. I swallowed it like it was the most precious thing that ever existed. Eros then pulled out with a satisfying smirk on his face.

The sound of hand rubbing against hardened skin told me that this was far from over. I crept my head around, noticing that his colleague was still standing right behind me.

He spat onto his hand, getting on his knees. Lubing up his dick with his saliva, he settled his hands on my thighs and yanked me to him with force. I had just about enough time to feel his shaft stretching my pussy lips and popping my hymen.

I wasn't a virgin anymore, and knowing that made me feel more important than I was. Arching his body over mine, I could feel his hot breath against my neck and his pecs pressing against my back.

Shivers running down my spine, I couldn't help but predict how much pain he was going to make me feel. He had to be over 10 inches long. I never thought a man could be so big, thick, and dominating.

And not long after, he started to pound in and out of me. A

smile crept up on my face. It was like a dream come true.

CHAPTER 3

The mafioso was pounding in and out of me, his balls slapping off my butt. Moaning, I couldn't imagine myself being anything different than their hucow. His dick erupted inside of me, sending rope after rope of salty and tasty come inside of me.

I clenched my walls around him tight. He tried pulling out, but it was lodged inside of me. I thought that what I did was going to piss him off and that he was going to punish me, but the smile on his face told me a different story.

He groaned, lowering his head. His lips were so close to my ear I could smell the minty smell coming out of his mouth. He glided his hand over the side of my neck as his dick sputtered one last rope of his dense and heavy milk inside of me.

The mafioso then murmured into my ear, "Tomorrow morning, you'll be someone much different."

Shivers ran down my spine. The direction I was taking for my life was irreversible and, yet, I was still going through with it. My walls were clenched so tight around his massive dick it was going to be almost impossible for him to pull out.

And yet, part of me knew he didn't mind that at all.

I could hear his controlled, but raggedy breathing as his dick softened up inside of me. His balls were still tight, but increasing in volume. With a shove of his hips, the man pulled out, leaving me gasping for air on the soil of the barn.

Skin friction noises right in front of me told me that things weren't quite over yet. I tilted my head up, finding out that Eligio was jacking off. The sight of me splayed on the floor, my body in pain, turned him on like nothing else could.

His hand was flying across his cock in a blur, his legs stiffening up as his balls pulled toward his groin. When his dick was throbbing again, I knew that more of his delicious come was going to be spurting out soon.

And one long rope after the other, he painted my face and body in white with it.

My whole body wasn't just in pain anymore, but also warm and sticky. I tried pulling my body back up, but the come glued to my skin was impeding me.

That and also the fact I didn't have more energy to burn after spending all of it in our sex.

Eros got on one knee, caressing my right cheek with his hand. As he locked his eyes with mine, he said, "Don't worry. Everything will be fine tomorrow morning. I can't wait to see until your body is even tastier than it is now."

I woke up the next morning feeling my body heavier than normal. I was in bed, covered by a comforter. I pushed it down with my hands and found out that I was much different than the person I used to be. My breasts were much bigger, my ass much curvier, and milk was seeping out of my nipples.

I swung my legs over the bed and got off of it, standing up. I padded over to the mirror on the wardrobe. I stood in front of it, noticing that I was naked. Naked like when I was born...

I bit my bottom lip when I realized that my skin was also smoother and glossier than before. I roamed my hands around my torso as I felt the curves of my new body.

Pulling my hand up, I pinched one of my nipples until a rope of milk squirted out of it, hitting the mirror. It ruined the perfect image I was seeing in it, but that was okay. I was pretty sure I could wipe it clean later.

I whirled around when I felt a pair of hands settling on my shoulders. I froze up right away as I realized that someone was eating me up with his eyes. They were the hands of a man so perfect that I couldn't even describe him. He dipped his head, making me feel the hot breath blowing out of his mouth.

"What did I tell you before that you were going to become someone much better than who you were?" He purred, nuzzling against my neck. I shivered as I squirmed against his dominance.

He lowered one of his hands as he put it against my right boob, toying with my nipple as he flicked his fingers over it. Each flick was like shooting shockwaves of pleasure through my whole body. He was making my knees wobble, and the look in his eyes that I could see through the reflection in the mirror showed me he didn't even care about that.

He ceased what he was doing for a moment, making me tilt my head up. I looked up as I found his eyes staring at me.

"Do you want to see one thing I can do with you now?" He asked, pinching my nipple until a line of milk sputtered out of it and splashed against the mirror.

"But that's not anything new. I already did that before you came in," I argued, noticing that he was smiling again.

"That's not the only thing I can do," he cooed into my ear as he put his hands on my shoulders again and turned me around. I was now in front of him and feeling a lot more exposed than ever before.

"And what is it that you can do?" I quizzed, realizing that he was shoving me against the mirror. I felt my back colliding against it and the milk, his body pressing against mine.

When he dipped his head again, I knew what he was going to do, and it turned me on more than I already was.

CHAPTER 4

It was Eligio, enclosing his lips around my nipple. He applied pressure against it as the milk started to spurt out inside his mouth. He shut his eyes, savoring my taste.

He lowered his hands to my waistline so that he could hold me in place, even though he didn't need to. Now that I was a hucow like all the others and also pregnant, I was his. I was forever his.

"Master, what are you doing?" I quizzed as I realized I was making a mistake by asking him that, but not because I thought he was going to punish me. The reason was much different than that.

I already knew the answer to my question.

And it wasn't just enough that he was milking me with his hungry mouth. Eligio also had to do something else. Gliding his hand down, he moved it over my belly before stopping it when he was going to find my clit. He kept it there, groping my skin like he couldn't have enough of it.

Eligio was making murmuring sounds as he continued to suck on my teat. Each time he pressed his lips against my nipple, line after line of milk squirted inside his mouth. His eyes were still closed as he showed me how much he was enjoying this.

I was still frozen where I was, moving my hand to his shoulders and then around them, loving the hardness of his muscles. Before this, my breast was heavy, but now it wasn't. He was thirsty for my milk, more so than I thought he was.

"Master...?" I moaned, my knees wobbling and my body falling to the floor like I didn't have legs anymore. My nipple escaped his mouth the moment that happened, plucking out of it.

I thought that was going to be enough to take him out of his stupor, but all he was doing was licking his lips over and over as he rushed back to me.

Crawling across the floor, he covered the distance between us like it was nothing. I tried to kick him away from me, but I wasn't strong enough. And it wasn't like I really wanted to do that anyway. The truth was that I was enjoying how rough he was being with me.

I shoved my hands against his shoulders as he climbed on top of me, pulling his head down until his lips wrapped around my other nipple. This time, he roamed his hand over my belly before finding my little clit. He drew circles on it with his finger and then he pinched it with two of them, making me moan and groan in pleasure.

I tried reopening my eyes and found his eyes staring right into mine. He was hungry, huffing. Beads of sweat were rolling down his cheeks as he kept rubbing his finger over my clit. I arched my back in response to the overload of pleasure he was rewarding me with, and I then smiled.

A moment later, he snuck two of his fingers inside my womb. He started to rub them inside it, measuring no effort as he kept on scrubbing them over my pussy walls. Eligio was hungry and thirsty, murmuring something with his mouth I couldn't hear.

Grinding his body against mine, it wasn't long until he was pushing his pants down to his knees. His cock came out free, bouncing up and down. As he continued to grind his body against mine, he grabbed my thighs and yanked my legs over his shoulders.

With his lips still wrapped around my nipple, the man started to suck out all the milk I had inside my boob. He was relentless, his fingers still inside my cunt, and it looked like he wasn't going to pull them out anytime soon.

He was pressing his hand against my pussy lips, more often than not pulling at them with his fingers.

Eligio stopped what he was doing a moment later, letting me catch my breath. I had closed my eyes before and now I reopened them. Noticing that he was staring straight into my eyes again, it was like I could almost read what he was thinking.

"I'm going to fuck you until you're crying," he promised, rubbing his finger over my clit again, making it feel hotter. It was bigger now than it was before. My belly wasn't like a bump yet, but I was pretty sure that in the months to come, it was going to change. After all, hucow bellies were supposed to get bigger faster than it was with normal women. It was something I needed to keep in mind at all times.

In no time at all, he yanked me again to him with all the strength of his arms. He pierced me with his massive dick, stretching my pussy walls again like they were nothing to him. Pain shot through my whole body in waves, making me arch my back.

"Oh God, oh God," I muttered, his hand flying to my mouth as he shut it.

I locked my eyes with his, a smile creeping up on his face. "I don't want to hear another peep." And hearing that, I couldn't help but feel I was making a mistake. Now that I was pregnant with his heir, he was going to keep me forever.

When they both left the farm, I was pretty sure they would take me with them, which meant not seeing Otis and Walter, who were still a mystery to me. I wanted to see how big they were and how juicy their bodies were when naked.

I just wanted to feel them inside of me, creaming in my womb and knocking me up right after I delivered these pretty little ones inside my belly. And yes, I was pretty sure it was going to be more than one.

I groaned, my body shaking as another wave of orgasm swept through me. He took his hand off my mouth, rolled over, putting his hand on his chest as he caught his breath. Moments later, he was already getting back to his feet, and drops of his milk were already leaking out of my cunt.

Noticing that, the next thing I did was get on my knees and stick my tongue out. I lapped up the small pool on the wooden floor of the room, smiling as I pushed up a finger in my cunt.

I couldn't lose another drop of his delicious sperm.

CHAPTER 5

And I didn't. That same day, at night, a pair of lips greeted me. They were pressing against mine. I reopened my eyes after falling asleep and dreaming that Walter and Otis were already back from their year-long trip.

I was lying in the bed, noticing that it was someone different this time who was in front of me. It was Otis, the same cowboy I was fantasizing about. He was smiling from ear to ear, his hand moving up and down against his crotch.

I licked my lips. Since becoming a hucow, I was always naked in the farmhouse. Other than going into the barn and then out of it, I was never allowed out, which was disappointing, but I wasn't going to whine about that.

He grabbed me by my armpits as he pulled me up. In a moment, my feet were back on the floor and I was standing. Just when I thought I was going to open my mouth and ask him what was happening, someone appeared behind me.

He pushed me against the bed as he made me lie down on it. My ass was pointed toward him, my legs parting as I invited him inside of me. Sweat drops were pooling on my forehead and I was feeling like I was heavier now than I was the day before. It could be just my imagination playing tricks on me, but it still looked like my belly was already bigger.

I shook that thought out of my mind when I felt his hands roaming over my asscheeks. He lowered his head until he was mere inches from my pussy. When he spoke, he let out his southern accent. "God, I love a cunt like yours."

He hissed a breath over my buttcheeks, his hands parting my legs wider than they were. He was making space, already planning on how he was going to penetrate me with his mighty cock.

Shivers ran down my spine when I felt something pressing against my mouth. I opened it wide and then wider when I realized it wasn't enough. In a moment, something round was going inside it.

It took me no moment to realize it was a ball gag. It was big. When something snapped behind my head, I knew that I wasn't even going to be allowed to scream.

Walter climbed over the bed, lowering his head until his lips were nibbling on my earlobe. When he stopped doing that, his tongue going back into his mouth, he murmured, "We are going to fuck you so hard you won't even be able to walk around when we are done."

I couldn't even shake my head to protest against that. It wasn't that I was even trying to do that, though. He shoved his hand against my neck, bringing it down against the bed. I could breathe, but just barely. He wasn't forcing me. Before I came here, we decided on a safeword I could use in case I felt like things were overwhelming.

He pulled my body up with his hands, forcing my ass to be level with his cock. He stroked it until it was hard and veiny. Moments later, he yanked me to him as he made sure he was going to penetrate me in one fell swoop.

He pierced my flesh like it was nothing. Less than a second later, he was balls deep, pressing against the end of my tunnel. It was moist, hot, and clenching around his hardness. It was the only thing I could do.

And then the ball gag popped out of my mouth.

The cowboy started to pound in and out of me while his friend grabbed my hair and shoved my head down to his cock. I had just about enough time to think about what was happening when I felt his dick stretching my lips beyond their limits.

He'd been lubricating his dick with his pre-come for so long he didn't even have to wait for me to do anything. In a moment, he was inside my throat and fucking it until it was stinging.

I tried to breathe, tried to feel more pleasure than pain, but it was impossible. I tried to match the cowboy behind me thrust for thrust, but just like I thought before, it was impossible.

My vision darkened as I thought I was going blind. Everything was happening so fast I didn't even realize when the cowboy in front of me yanked out my ball gag. All I could still remember was his cock barging through my lips and getting lodged inside my throat.

If breathing before was difficult, now it was even more so. I didn't have much time to reflect on that, though. The cowboys' matched their rhythms, each of them torturing my holes and making me orgasm over and over, my body so tired and in pain that I thought I was going to pass out. If that happened, I'd fall into a coma and I didn't think I'd be able to get out of it.

Their dicks started to convulse inside of me, pumping out rope after rope of their come. It was dripping out of both of my holes when they finally pulled out with a popping sound, both at the same time – almost as if they'd been doing this all of their lives, and always together, too.

They then switched up places to make sure that each got a taste of me. More tired than I'd ever been in my life, I fell limp on the mattress and closed my eyes.

The last thing I saw was those cowboys opening the door of the room and trotting out. Otis and Walter would be back for more and, until then, I was going to be waiting…

The End

Looking for the first 4 books in the series? Download them

here:

1. Cowboys' Lucky Age Gap

2. Cowboys' Naughty Age Gap

3. Cowboys' Christmas Age Gap

4. Cowboys' Medical Age Gap

Lastly, leave a review if you liked this book. It really helps me.

SNEAK PEEK: COWBOYS' LUCKY AGE GAP

Fertile First Time Thanksgiving Story (Hucow Milking Farm - 1)

Perhaps everything would be so much easier if that hunk of a man wasn't seated across from me. We were in the dining room, and I wasn't alone.

His colleague was also with us, picking up a glass of wine and taking a sip from it. His eyes were locked with mine and it was like he was trying to read my mind.

I wasn't trying to read his mind, but I was ogling him without making it obvious I was doing that. I had no idea if he was picking that up, but he smiled and I could see the beautifulness of his super white teeth.

I was just checking him out, wishing I could be in his arms. They looked so strong, confident, veins popping out where I could more easily see them, hair in all the right places, and his skin tanned by the light of the sun. I'd been fantasizing about him since coming here.

And it wasn't just Walter's arms that made my pussy wet, but also his face. And more specifically, his lips.

I wouldn't say that they were big, but they look just right and I knew that if I were kissing them now, I'd be tasting how sweet they were.

His face was chiseled and looked perfect. He groomed his full, thick beard every day, and it looked sharp without making him look gay.

It gave him that extra spice of manliness I always craved in a man. Looking down slightly, I also loved how his beard transitioned to his neck. I could just imagine myself lying in his bed with him and cradling my head in the crook of his neck. I was pretty sure he would love it if I did that.

But something was impeding me from doing that, and it was the fact that I was a virgin. I didn't know much about these two guys, but I knew that they craved women that had a lot more experience.

I didn't want to disappoint them or myself.

His blond hair seemed to draw my attention to him, and I couldn't control that I was ogling it too. It was short, a bit bigger at the top, and even shorter at the sides. I had no idea if he got his hair cut often, but it was always sharp. This wasn't the first time I was checking him out, after all.

His eyes were icy blue and I suddenly found myself entranced by them. His eyes showed me that behind his tough persona, he was a free-spirited and extroverted man. I didn't need that to tell me that was what he was like, but it was great having that confirmation again.

Seated beside him was his colleague. He was forking a piece of meat on his plate, and I noticed the veins popping out on his forearms. His skin was also white, but just as tanned.

He didn't have a full beard like Walter, but his stubble actually made him look sexier. I could just imagine what it would be like to be grazing my hands over his chin and jawline, feeling the roughness of his skin.

And go to the next page for more books like this one.

BOOKS BY THIS AUTHOR

SERIES - FAVORITE HUCOWS

1. First Time in the Barn: A Fertile Harem Story

2. First Time in the Pen: A Fertile Harem Story

3. First Time in the Shed: A Fertile Harem Story

4. First Time in the Tractor: A Fertile Harem Story

5. First Time on the Haystack: A Fertile Harem Story

SERIES - FERTILE ONLY

1. Bumping the Teacher: A Hucow Mafia First Time Story

2. Bumping the Midwife: A Hucow Mafia First Time Story

3. Bumping the Farmhand: A Hucow Mafia First Time Story

4. Bumping the Sinner: A Hucow Mafia First Time Story

SERIES - HUCOW FOR WHITE COLLARS

1. Milked by the Lawyers: A First Time Bimbo Ménage Story

2. Milked by Doctors: A First Time Bimbo Ménage Story

3. Milked by Engineers: A First Time Bimbo Ménage Story

4. Milked by Directors: A First Time Bimbo Ménage Story

5. Milked by Managers: A First Time Bimbo Ménage Story
24

And you can also get these fertile hucow mega bundles:

Creaming the Bimbo: A Fertile Hucow MEGA Collection

Milked by Cowboys: A Hucow Milking MEGA Bundle

Milked for Christmas: 15 First Time Hucow Stories

Fertile Leakers: 10 Milking Stories

Milked, Shared and Used: 16 Stories of Milking Ladies

ABOUT THE AUTHOR

Leandra's Camilli's obsession? Writing dirty, steamy stories that will make you drool. She loves her Alpha males, hucows, sissies, and futas. If you're looking for that kind of book, you've found the right author page.

With a cup of coffee on her table and warm socks on, she writes almost every day. Leandra Camilli's been present in several top 100 categories in the store, and she always finishes her stories.